Mr. Wellington

Mr. Wellington

David Rabe

Illustrations by
Robert Andrew Parker

A NEAL PORTER BOOK
ROARING BROOK PRESS
NEW YORK

A Neal Porter Book

Published by Roaring Brook Press

Roaring Brook Press is a division of Holtzbrinck Publishing

Holdings Limited Partnership

175 Fifth Avenue, New York, New York 10010

www.roaringbrookpress.com

Distributed in Canada by H. B. Fenn and Company Ltd.

Cataloging-in-Publication Data is on file at the Library of Congress

ISBN: 978-1-59643-328-1

Roaring Brook Press books are available for special promotions and premiums.

For details contact: Director of Special Markets, Holtzbrinck Publishers.

First Edition May 2009

Book design by Jennifer Browne

Printed in March 2009 in the United States of America by Worzalla,

Stevens Point, Wisconsin

2   4   6   8   10   9   7   5   3   1

For
Michael, Jason, Lily

CHAPTER ONE

 Mystery. And the dark of night coming down all around him. And the squirrel didn't know where he was. The cold was getting deep inside him, and no matter where he looked he saw nothing familiar. Trees, yes. And grass. And more trees. And dirt. And fallen branches, and bark and more trees and more grass. But none that were his tree. The one where his home was. Where he lived with his mother and his brothers and sisters. Where he'd been playing roughly with his brother. Feeling strong. As strong as anything in the world. Pushing, tugging, nipping, even when his mother told them both to stop. She was going to go out and forage for acorns, as she always did. Didn't they want their acorns?

He wanted acorns but he didn't want to stop playing, because he could beat his brother and he knew it and his brother had nipped him, and he wanted to get even and get in an extra nip. The last nip. And so when his mother's big gray tail sailed from sight as she scampered over the edge of their nest and off down, down, down, he just couldn't quite stop wanting to fight. To play. So he'd turned around and eyed his brother with a look that was like a little bite, and then made a crooked face. When that hadn't been enough to get the wrestling going again, he'd hopped over and delivered a poke and a nip and fled. But he fled too quickly and not exactly straight off down the branch as planned, but too much to the side and too fast and too steep, so that his front feet barely found bark, and he was unable to hang on and keep from flipping out into the air. Into nothing to grab or claw or climb except a leaf or two that simply blew away and did nothing to stop or slow him. And everything around him raced past in a long and longer blur of green and brown and blue until the biggest bump of his life took all his breath away and with it all the color everywhere other than black.

And when he woke up he screamed right away for his mother, but she didn't come. He screamed for his brothers and sisters, but they didn't scream back. His mother always had come when he screamed like that. Once he'd gone running down a branch with her and when he

looked and she was gone, he screamed and she came right to him. But not this time. It scared him to scream and hear the scream, and it scared him that she didn't come. He'd run then, even though his head hurt and he felt a little strange. He ran to find her because she had to be nearby. He didn't know when that had been, but it seemed long, long ago. He saw trees that looked like his tree, but when he tried to climb them they weren't his tree and he knew it. He went under bushes and through brushes and every now and then he screamed to call her, but she didn't come. And every now and then he just screamed.

But now it was night and dark and the cold was getting inside him where the fear already was, and he was hungry, so very hungry. He found an acorn but he couldn't get it open with his tiny teeth. They were too little and the acorn was too hard, and he was so tired and sick. He wanted to sleep but couldn't because he was scared that something bad would happen if he slept out in the dark away from his brothers and sisters, and out in the open anything could see him and sneak up and . . .

Warm, he thought. Warm. I want to be warm, and I want to eat and I want to ... He just stopped and sat. The spot he had come upon was somehow warmer than where he'd been, though it didn't have any grass or weeds, and it was hard. There was dust on it and pebbles, and it was hard, though it was warmer than anything else, so he sat there even when the roaring noise came and daylight seemed to pour over him. He just didn't care or understand, but at least he was warm. And then a strange force came and sort of nudged him, and the force was warmer than the spot he'd been on even though the force was moving him off the spot. The next thing he felt was tree bark under his little claws, but he couldn't climb and it wasn't his tree. How was this happening? The way he was being pushed around and moved and picked up and set down. . . Then the warmth went away and the squirrel hung there, knowing it was useless to go up this strange tree because his mother wasn't up there, and his brothers and sisters weren't up there. But the warmth came back and carried him down to the dirt and grass, where it set

him down and left him and then came back and pushed at him as if to shove him into the dark forest, where bad things waited and where it was cold and the dirt and grass were cold, and as the warmth left again, he screamed. It wasn't his mother, but it was warm, and he screamed and when it came back this time, he grabbed it with both front paws and both back paws, and he put his little claws into the warmth as much as he could and he hung on. He chattered to make his point, hoping his noise would explain that he couldn't let go. He wouldn't let go. The warmth was warm and he was cold. He had to hang on with every little muscle he had. And then the warmth changed somehow. It opened. It let him in like a hole in a tree, or a nest, and he crawled in and curled his tail up around him, and the warmth was like sunshine in the middle of the night, and he went to sleep. Hungry and thirsty and scared still, he slept.

CHAPTER TWO

When the headlight on his bicycle lit up the squirrel in the middle of the road, Jonathan turned to go around it, but as he rode past, he noticed that the squirrel didn't move. He pedaled a few more strokes, and then started to worry that a car might come along and run over the little animal. It was strange the way it was just sitting there and not moving. He circled back and aimed his headlight and saw that the squirrel was a baby. Just sitting there on that road with the sun down and the light all but gone. Jonathan was on his way home from the lake, where he'd gone to take photographs for a school project, and was hungry and a little late for dinner. But

then, he knew that dinner wasn't all that organized because his mom and dad were away for the weekend, and it was just Jonathan and his older brother who was home for a few days from college.

After watching the squirrel for a second, Jonathan decided that maybe he should just try to move it off the road. Wheeling his bike to take advantage of the head-light, he approached the squirrel. Its head was bowed over like it was staring at the ground, and it looked sad or worried or scared or something not very good. Where were the other squirrels? Didn't it have a family? He pushed at it carefully, nudging it off the dusty pavement, over the few scattered pebbles and onto the grass. At least it should be off the road. The squirrel just let itself be moved and it didn't fight back or try to bite or resist, and Jonathan started to worry that it might be hurt or sick. How long had it been out here alone like this? he wondered. What would happen to it? There were dogs around, and he had even seen foxes darting across this road. Maybe he should put the squirrel in a tree, he thought, and he very carefully reached and lifted the little body so tiny and frail and soft, which just kind of melted into his fingers. He lifted it up to a nearby tree and placed it against the trunk maybe five feet up in the air and the squirrel grabbed hold with its little claws. Jonathan thought, Good. He'll climb up and go to the top and do what squirrels do at night. Whatever that was. He didn't really know. He guessed they had nests or maybe hollow places in the tree where they—

He stopped thinking about it because the little squirrel hadn't moved. It was just hanging there on the side of the tree, looking like it might fall off at any second. He moved his bike closer so the light would let him see clearly, and it looked like its little legs were shaking. Fearing the squirrel would fall, Jonathan picked it off the tree, and put it down in the grass. He had to get home. He looked down at the tiny little body in the grass and thought that maybe he should at least get it deeper into the weeds and

DAVID RABE

trees along the road before he left, so he put his toe against the squirrel and gently shoved the squirrel a few inches and then a foot and the squirrel sort of skidded and hopped once and then stopped. Jonathan pulled his foot away and turned to walk back to his bike on the road and the squirrel screamed. It was a sad, lost little high-pitched scream, and when Jonathan stepped back toward it, the squirrel grabbed hold of his sneaker with all four feet and claws and hung on. Now he didn't know what to

do, and when he lifted his foot as if to shake the squirrel loose, the little animal rose with his foot, clinging to his sneaker. It took him a minute for Jonathan to realize he couldn't walk like this or ride his bike with this squirrel holding on to his sneaker, so he bent and untied the laces and slid the sneaker off his foot. The cold of the ground came right into his foot then, through his sock and into his skin, and as he felt the cold from the ground, the squirrel scrambled sideways and up onto the top of his sneaker and then plunged inside. It went in headfirst right where his foot had been, and it curled there on its side like it had gone into a cave, and its tail, like a little flag or blanket, fell over it.

So that's the way Jonathan walked home then, holding his sneaker in his hands with the squirrel curled up and sleeping inside it, and with every step the cold ground went into his foot, icy and deep, just as it had been working its way inside the little squirrel and making him colder and colder until Jonathan happened along.

CHAPTER THREE

 With his head covered up by the curl of his tail, the squirrel felt almost as though he was in the middle of a big jump. He hadn't jumped that he knew of. He'd just grabbed hold and hung on. He was too tired to jump even if he wanted to. But still, there he was, full of all that jumping feeling, like when he was with his brother sometimes and he ran and he wanted to get from one place to another quickly, or if something was in his way, and so he'd tighten all his leg muscles, and then let them go free, jumping light and fast. And that was what he was feeling now, only it was bumpy. He went up and down, and rocked from side to side

with the up-and-down way the warmth was moving, and the side-to-side way it was moving. It was the warmth that was making it all happen.

He peeked then, nudging his tail aside so he could see past it, hoping to see something, maybe even the warmth, but there was only dark. And the dark seemed to be bouncing all over the place. High up there were black streaks that made him think of trees and feel sad. He had no idea where he was going. But he wasn't where he should be. He knew that he wasn't in the trees. Past the black streaks that made him think of trees he saw the big round light that his mother and older brother had said was their "friend," warning them to stay in their trees in the night. But he hadn't obeyed. He hadn't disobeyed either. He'd only played when maybe he shouldn't, and he had fallen. Maybe he was still falling.

He pushed his tail over his eyes. He was thirsty, and hungry, too, but mainly now he was tired. He worried about falling asleep, because there might be something he should try to do. He tried to think what it was. Run? Jump? Scratch? Bite?

The warmth was all he had, even though it bounced. Exhausted and lost, he floated into a long, dark tunnel. He could not keep his eyes open. Where was he going? Where? In the strange, dreamy softness, he settled, he slept.

CHAPTER FOUR

 When Jonathan walked in the front door, he smelled food cooking. His older brother, Vincent, was frying hamburgers as Jonathan entered the kitchen and said, "I have a baby squirrel."

"What?" said Vincent, sounding almost annoyed. "You're kidding."

Jonathan held up the sneaker, and Vincent took a long look at the squirrel inside. "How did he get in there?"

"He crawled in. He was down by the corner at Hilltop and our street, and he was just sitting in the middle of the road."

The little gray-brown body snuggled as deep in the

hollow of the sneaker as it could go. It lay in a kind of self-tied knot, with its tail looped over it like a blanket.

"He's probably hungry, don't you think?" Jonathan asked.

"And thirsty, too, I guess. How long was he out there?"

"I don't know. How would I know?"

Because Jonathan had his hands full holding the sneaker and squirrel, Vincent poured milk into a small bowl and held it out by the sneaker. Jonathan shook the sneaker and the squirrel stirred and reversed itself and peeked over the edge at the milk, but then he sank back.

"He doesn't look so good, does he?"

"Do you think he's hurt or sick?" Jonathan wondered.

"Maybe it's just that squirrels don't like milk. Let's try something else."

He dumped the milk in the sink, then washed the bowl before filling it with water.

"What about nuts? They eat nuts, right?"

"Sure. Of course."

"Do we have any nuts?"

"Walnuts or something, I bet."

Vincent held the little cup of water close to the sneaker and the squirrel edged out, leaning a little and looking like it was thinking over the idea of water.

"I'll bet he's thirsty."

And then the squirrel lunged for the water and Jonathan flinched. After so much stillness the sudden movement was scary, and his hands jumped away from the sneaker, and the squirrel and sneaker both fell to the floor, where they made a loud thump.

As the two boys stared down in shock, the squirrel, looking worried, retreated into the sneaker. And he seemed to dig in even deeper this time.

"I didn't expect him to jump like that," said Jonathan, bending to pick up the sneaker. "I hope I didn't hurt him."

"Maybe we should just let him rest awhile."

"Poor little guy."

"I'll grind up some nuts."

Knowing they had to put him somewhere safe, they decided to get an old dog cage up from the basement and place it in the bathroom attached to the guest room. The cage was made of wire with holes too small for a squirrel to crawl through, not that the little creature was likely to go anywhere since it didn't want to leave the sneaker. The bathroom had a door and there was a door to the guest room and the cage had a door, too. They could all be shut.

Vincent found a bag of walnuts in the pantry and ground them up in a blender. Jonathan put water into an old jar lid so the edge would be low enough for the squirrel to reach over. Vincent put the nuts in a small bowl and then more water in another small bowl. Once the dog cage was in the bathroom, they put everything inside. Then Jonathan knelt and, carefully, set the sneaker with the squirrel on the floor of the cage. Vincent crouched down, and together they looked in at the squirrel huddled under the sweep of its tail, eyes closed, little body puffing up and down with breathing.

"Look at him; he's so sleepy," said Vincent.

"How long do you think he was out there in the dark alone?"

"Probably awhile."

"He must have been so scared. He's so little."

"Maybe he got lost. Or his mom got hit by a car."

"Do you think it could have been out there alone for more than one night?"

"Out in the dark and the cold."

"With things that might eat you."

"Actually, he probably couldn't have survived a whole night. So whatever happened, probably happened today."

"The poor little guy."

"Look how sleepy he is."

"You know what?" said Jonathan. "I have an idea."

"What?"

"I'll be right back." When Jonathan returned, he brought an old cardboard box with one end cut out so that it took on the shape of a cave. Placing it inside the dog cage, he fit it over the water and the nuts, and over the sneaker with the squirrel inside, keeping the open end toward them so they could still look in and see him.

"He seemed to want a hiding place," said Jonathan.

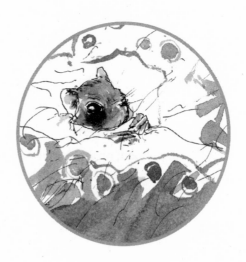

CHAPTER FIVE

The squirrel floated along in a strange, dreamy softness, falling down a long, dark tunnel that he recognized as the one that waited at the end of each day of his life. It came when he could no longer keep his eyes open, and it had come even today. It was sleep.

But suddenly there was bright light everywhere, and he looked around. It was warm and the sights were strange. Big round blurry presences came and went like the wind through the branches or a hole in a tree. There was noise, and some of it was chatter, a little like squirrels talking, but nothing he could understand. He was hungry and dizzy but no longer so cold, and when the soft hole in which he was dozing shook, he stirred and looked out at the blurry spheres that came and went with the sounds, and there was also a circle of something that reminded him of water and he was thirsty but it smelled bad. That was the other thing. The smells were strong and they felt dangerous. Part of him was very worried and felt he should flee, that he was in danger. If he hadn't been so weary, he'd have been terrified. The smells were unknown, and they alarmed him, and then the white was gone and what came floating near was water. It looked like water and smelled like water and he wanted it so he just went out for it, and something happened that reminded him of falling from the tree and losing everything, and it was like little claws running up through him as he went down and landed hard with a thump. Only this time the dark didn't come taking away everything. But he felt scared and he turned and curled back into the warm soft hole that was still there. He went as deep as he could go, as deep and as far, and then he just shut his eyes. He was worn out. So tired he didn't know what to do except sleep. He had to sleep. Just sleep.

That was all he knew for the longest time until he awoke again and smelled water and smelled food. Though he worried his actions might lead to another fall, he was too hungry and thirsty to resist. He ventured carefully from the warmth and found that the water was there and he could drink. The food was nuts; not his favorites, not acorns, but good, and he curled his hind feet under him and leaned in to the nuts and nibbled and chewed.

CHAPTER SIX

 "Vincent! Vincent!" Jonathan galloped into his brother's room, where Vincent, lying on his bed, looked up from a big book. "Come, look! He's eating!"

"Really?"

They hurried to the guest room, but then slowed and slipped quietly into the bathroom. They crouched, peering together into the cardboard cave, where the little squirrel was bowed over the bowl of nuts, ducking his head in and plucking out nuts and chewing.

"That's good, huh? He's eating. That's a good sign."

"Yeah."

"Well," said Vincent. "Well, look at you. Looks like

the right kid found you, and you're going to get a second chance. Looks like you got lucky, Mr. Wellington."

"They like raisins, too."

"How do you know?"

"I looked on the Internet."

"You did? And you got that?"

"Yeah. I searched squirrels and they like mangos and raisins."

"I don't know about mangos, but I bet we have raisins."

As they went to the kitchen, Jonathan asked, "What was it you called him? Mr. Something?"

"Mr. Wellington. He needs a name. Do you like it?"

"I do. But I don't know why."

"I don't either. It just popped into my head, but I think it's his tail. It's like this big plume, you know. And there was a famous general, the Duke of Wellington, and he wore a hat like that—with a big plume. He defeated Napoleon in a big battle and saved his country."

"Mr. Wellington."

"Unless you want to name him something else."

"No. I like it."

Late that night, Jonathan was restless. He tried to sleep, but he kept thinking about Mr. Wellington and how he probably wouldn't be saving any countries. Jonathan could only hope Mr. Wellington would be able to save himself. He had seemed so vulnerable and delicate. Even frail.

Climbing from bed, he settled down in front of his computer. Once he typed in "Help for baby squirrels," the screen surprised him with the number of destinations that came up. As he began to study and sort them, one site led to another until he came to one called "Small Mammals in Distress." That site linked him up to another, where people who might help were listed state by state. Seeing how many of these people, called "wildlife rehabilitators," there were, and how much information was available, alarmed Jonathan. He worried that Mr. Wellington was delicate and complicated, that there were issues involved in his well-being that neither he nor his brother had considered because they did not know enough to even think of them, whatever they were.

Wanting to look in on Mr. Wellington, Jonathan stopped outside the door. He was worried that turning the light on would frighten the squirrel. About to go back, he realized that if he put the hall light on with both the guest room and bathroom doors open, light would spill gently in over the cage. He was right, and sneaking in, he was able to see Mr. Wellington lying motionless beneath the swirl of his tail, his eyes closed and transformed into dark little slits. In the shadows, Jonathan suddenly feared the little squirrel wasn't really breathing and sleeping like he thought, but was sick and dying or even dead. Jonathan leaned closer and squinted to see better, but finally had to reach in and touch the little body to make certain he could feel the tiny motion of the tiny belly breathing.

Back at the computer, he read all kinds of warnings and instructions. The more he read, the more it seemed that he and his brother could never care for Mr. Wellington without help. Jonathan was starting to believe that he needed help from one of these people who knew all about squirrels. They could advise him, and then he would know how to treat Mr. Wellington so that he could keep him and make sure he got well.

Jonathan eventually found the e-mail address and phone number of a wildlife rehabber near where he lived, a woman in a small town about five miles away. He wrote her about everything that had happened and included his e-mail address and phone number before sending it off. He read more about Small Mammals in Distress, and wondered why he still didn't feel sleepy. He wanted to tell his brother what he'd learned and what he'd done, but when he got to Vincent's room, he saw that the lights were out and knew that Vincent must be sound asleep. It was the middle of the night. He paced around outside the door, and then went to the big window in the living room and looked out at the dark sky and slight moon, which was distant and covered in clouds but still shining through. It looked cold out there.

At last, he began to feel sleepy. But before going to bed, he ground up some more nuts, put fresh water in the little bowl, and because there had been numerous warnings about baby squirrels' needing to be kept warm, he draped a big blue blanket over the cage and turned the heat up high in the guest room.

CHAPTER SEVEN

 Mr. Wellington woke in a deep, deep darkness. And it was hot. He was still tired. Still so very tired, but less hungry, though he did want to eat. It was time to eat and he could smell food and water close by, so he roused himself and went to them. He nibbled the nuts and sipped the water and sat back before leaning in to nibble and sip some more.

He sat for a while at the front of his nest, peering at the darkness in which there was nothing but the smell that made him feel he was in some kind of danger but he didn't know what it was. It was just a strange smell, a smell that made him nervous when there was nothing

really to be nervous about that he knew of. But everything was so strange and there was so much that he didn't know. And something dangerous was near. He felt it, smelled it, and sometimes it moved closer. It moved very close and then it went away. He remembered a faint light that fell over him, as he slept, and then went away. But he could-stay awake. Not even to run or hide if he needed protection. He was just too tired. And hot. It was so hot. He'd eaten. It was time to sleep. Even if it wasn't time to sleep, he had to sleep, and he made his way back and curled up again in the little padded circle of warmth he had found, where he felt safe. The padded circle that had carried him in from the cold, that had brought him food and water. It was his now, his sleeping place. He arched his tail up and let it fall down like the softest breeze floating down to cover him, its light, whispering touch like his own soothing voice telling him not to be afraid and to just sleep. Not that he could have stopped himself from sleeping. He blinked twice more and then that was that, and the night went on and on. Full of sleep and nibbles and a little nervousness. Moments spent peering out of his padded little soft circle at the dark, and long, long periods during which weariness and sleep were gentle and sweet and safe.

CHAPTER EIGHT

Saturday morning, Vincent drove off to have breakfast with some high school friends who, like him, were home for the weekend. Jonathan watched him go, and then paid a visit to Mr. Wellington. He removed the blue blanket and tossed it into the corner. Mr. Wellington appeared okay but was deeply asleep. Jonathan checked his e-mail to see if the wildlife rehabber had written back to him, but she hadn't. He watched some television and jumped to the phone every time it rang. The first two calls were annoying telemarketers, whom he listened to for a moment and then hung up on. A friend of his mother's called. Then his parents telephoned, just wanting to

check in and make sure everything was all right. He decided not to tell them about Mr. Wellington, because they would be home the next evening and he wanted them to be able to see Mr. Wellington before learning that he was in the guest room.

When his friend Andrew called, Jonathan explained about Mr. Wellington. Pretty soon Andrew and his sister, Missy, were dropped off by their parents so they could meet him in person. They all got down on the bath-room floor while Mr. Wellington just sat near the sneaker, looking tired. Jonathan reached in and stroked Mr. Wellington with a finger, and Mr. Wellington barely stirred. Or if he stirred at all, it was peacefully, as if he recalled the cold and the night and the road and the warmth of Jonathan's sneaker that had saved him.

After they left, Jonathan checked his e-mail, but still had no response. It had been fun showing Mr. Wellington to his friends, but he hadn't liked the way the squirrel behaved. Entering quietly, he bent over to peer in through

the open front of the cardboard box inside the cage. He saw instantly that Mr. Wellington was gone. The box was empty. The cage was empty. He looked inside the box again, even though he had no doubts. Both doors to the bathroom were closed, so Mr. Wellington could not have gotten out of the bathroom. Jonathan was positive he'd entered carefully, watching the floor, just in case, so he was sure Mr. Wellington had not run out. The toilet lid was down, so Mr. Wellington could not have fallen in there. But where was he? He searched the room again, every corner, every inch. Where was he? And then his eyes went back to the blanket that was heaped in the corner. Carefully, he approached and reached down and patted the miniature hills and cloudlike puffs. The blanket was like a blue hillside full of crevices and caves and Jonathan started to search them one at a time. He shifted the folds and looked in the doubled-over sections. He examined the layers overlapping each other like the petals in a big flower, reaching here, reaching there, lifting one loose end and then another, until he picked one up and there was Mr. Wellington, sound asleep on his side in the piled-up blue of the blanket.

Jonathan felt very relieved as he lowered the blanket back over Mr. Wellington. Then, wanting to make sure there was room for air to come and go so Mr. Wellington could breathe, Jonathan fluffed the material up a little, creating a kind of vent. As he straightened, thinking that the next thing he should do was remove the food and water bowls from the cage and place them on the floor near the blanket, he saw a little hand with tiny, gleaming dark fingers at the end of a small, furry arm reach out from the vent he'd created. As he watched, the fingers closed on the edge of the vent and pulled it down, tugging the covers back the way they had been, the way Mr. Wellington wanted them.

CHAPTER NINE

He'd had to do it. That was all he knew. The world was still hot and there was light and it was very, very bright, and the smells that made him worry were getting stronger, becoming overwhelming as he woke up with a surge of energy and desire that, after eating some nuts and eating some raisins and drinking a little water, and then a little more water, drove him to press against the silver branches keeping him away from whatever was beyond them. He pressed and clawed and scrambled, and for an instant, as he fought, he felt that the life he'd lost in the cold and dark awaited him now, that the world into which he'd been born was soon

to be regained just outside this force holding him back.

But it wasn't. Once he squeezed past the wire branches and out into the waiting space, he found no wind, no acorns, no leaves, no high branches wavering in the breeze, no trees to climb. Just flat, flat hard dirt, like stones really, and big rock walls without the slightest gap in them and nothing soft except a kind of fallen pile of sky. At least its color was the color of the sky collected all

in a bunch. And he'd worn himself out, fighting and struggling to get where he was. The piled-up sky was puffy and soft and because he needed to be warm, he found a hole somewhat like the soft roundness that had saved him and that he'd slept in and now had left behind. Wiggling in, he turned on his side and he felt weak, almost sick. Everything wore him out and left him feeling nervous and worried, and the nervousness and worry wore him out even worse, so that he had to sleep, and sleep seemed to take the worry away. His eyes closed and he saw nothing, and his brain gave up and he thought nothing. Dark and sleep. That was all he knew. Sleep and warmth and nothing else except a mild worry as if something were growling at him from far, far away, until something changed and he felt cold. It was like when the wind would blow in through a hole in the nest where he had once slept in a tree, only he wasn't in a tree and his nest wasn't really a nest. He didn't know what it was, except he was in it and it was soft and over him and something had moved to let the cold come in to touch him and he reached out, hoping to find something to close the cold out, and he found a part of his nest that wasn't really a nest, but still he could pull it down. He closed his fingers and tugged his nest back the way he wanted it, shutting out the wind with whatever it was he was nestled in, and back to sleep he fell.

CHAPTER TEN

 Sunday morning, the telephone rang at about ten-thirty. It was the wildlife rehabber. Her name was Sandy, and she offered to take over the care of Mr. Wellington if they would deliver him to her house. She wanted to talk to Jonathan's parents, and when she learned they were away, she asked to speak to Vincent, because he was older, so Vincent got on the kitchen phone while Jonathan went to the extension in the living room. She asked about Mr. Wellington's size and what he was eating. She said that, based on the description in Jonathan's e-mail, he was probably not a baby squirrel, but a "juvenile," a kind of teenager. She said that walnuts were

okay, but he would do better if given acorns. Did they know of any acorn trees near where he lived? Milk was bad, water was good. Raisins were good. She'd never heard of any squirrels eating mangos. Where would they get them? Also, it was important to understand that he was wild. He was a wild animal who belonged in the wild. She wanted to make sure they both understood that as nice as they were being to Mr. Wellington, it was very stressful for him to be around them.

"But why?" Jonathan asked. "We're taking good care of him."

"Because he's wild. He belongs outside in the trees and with other squirrels. Living that life. Your smells, the smells in the house, the sounds, all of it is unnatural for him and—I'm sorry to say—threatening." As she talked, Jonathan had trouble listening because everything she was saying sounded like she believed the only good thing they could do for Mr. Wellington would be to give him to her, because of all the knowledge she had about squirrels and the treatment they required, the special foods she could provide, which would give Mr. Wellington the best kind of nutrition. It made him sad, and a little angry. He didn't see why she couldn't just tell him what to do and give him some of the special food. Vincent was saying that he thought he understood, but that he wanted to talk things over with Jonathan. Everybody said good-bye, and they hung up.

Jonathan hurried to the kitchen where Vincent stood by the phone very serious, very thoughtful. After a second he said, "Well."

"Let's go look for some acorns," Jonathan said.

They both knew where a large oak tree stood in a field below their home, and they wandered around its base, not saying much. No acorns had fallen. There were twigs, scattered stones, clumps of dirt, a few leaves, but no acorns.

"Maybe we should just give him some more walnuts," Vincent said after a while.

"Let's look a little bit longer."

"Not that we should keep him even if we find some acorns."

"She said they'd be good for him to eat."

"She said a lot of other things, too. You heard her. It's very stressful for him to be here."

"I don't understand that."

"No?"

Suddenly, thinking he saw an acorn, Jonathan shouted, "What's that?" and bent toward something round, brown, and shiny that turned out to be a stone. He stood up slowly.

"The part that made sense to me," said Vincent, "was when she talked about how we don't think of squirrels as wild animals like tigers and lions and elephants or wolves. I mean, wild like that, but he really is just as wild. He belongs out there. He's a wild animal. I mean, really a wild animal. "

"I was thinking he could live with us."

"Even if he was unhappy?"

"Maybe he wouldn't be, though. What about that?" He looked around and shook his head. Why weren't there any acorns?

"The other thing that really made sense to me was where she said that if we wanted to understand the kind of stress he's feeling here—no matter how nice we are to him—we should try to imagine how one of us would feel if we were lost in the dark woods. All alone. No other people. No idea how we'd gotten there. Just all alone and miles from everything we knew and no idea how to get back. That's how bad he feels here."

"I guess I didn't do the right thing bringing him home."

"No, you did."

"Why? If he's so unhappy?"

"Jonathan, c'mon. She explained that, too. You were on the phone."

They'd stopped looking for acorns and were sitting in

the grass. Jonathan picked up a small stone and tossed it.

"What'd she say about what you might have done if it was daylight?" his brother asked.

"She said that in the daylight maybe I could have sat and watched to see if his mother came for him when he yelled for her. That would have been the best thing in the daylight."

"But that wasn't the way it was—it wasn't day. It was night."

"I know."

"At night in the dark like that, when it's getting cold, his mother probably would never have come for him, because they usually don't in the night."

"It's sad, huh? That mother squirrels don't usually come down after it's dark like that even if they hear the baby crying."

"Well, it's dangerous. So you did the right thing, because he probably would have died before morning."

Jonathan said nothing, though he nodded. He stood

and started trudging back up through the field toward their house.

"You did a good thing, Jonathan," Vincent called after him.

Jonathan kept going, but when his brother caught up, he said, "You know, I was coming back from taking those pictures of the lake for this project at school and that was okay, I'd done okay; but I wasn't feeling very good for other reasons. I was feeling bad, sort of. I was feeling sort of, what's the point? You know. You know that feeling—what's the point in anything? So I'm in that kind of mood, and then I come around a corner and the next thing I know, I'm there to save this baby squirrel."

CHAPTER ELEVEN

 He was sick. He woke up and fell back to sleep. Following smells, he staggered to the water and the nuts and raisins and he ate some, but just getting to them and just eating a little wore him down so much he could barely get back to the hole where he slept, and somewhere along the way he faltered and stopped and sat there staring off, drowsy and sad and unable to move. Just sitting and staring and sort of sleeping. After a while he stirred and struggled on to the soft blue piles of whatever they were, and he fell down into them, and down again he went, into a deep, deep sleep that seemed like something new and strange and

not exactly sleep at all. It seemed to be something that would not let him go, something from which he might not wake up.

CHAPTER TWELVE

 As soon as Sandy touched Mr. Wellington, she knew something was wrong. She'd been joking about Jonathan and Vincent transporting Mr. Wellington in an old milk crate with no top and nothing in it except for the blue blanket. Vincent had driven them over in the car he would take back to college. Jonathan sat holding Mr. Wellington in the passenger seat, while his bike was packed in the back. Vincent had a big History paper to finish before a morning class at school, so the plan was that he would drop Jonathan and Mr. Wellington off at Sandy's and then drive on, leaving Jonathan to bicycle home.

As soon as they'd come back into the house after searching for acorns, they'd begun to worry that Mr. Wellington was acting slow and tired. And then over the next hour, he'd grown more listless and uninterested in anything. After calling Sandy and being told to drive over quickly, Jonathan had just picked up the blanket from the bathroom floor with Mr. Wellington's little body cradled inside. Vincent had stayed only long enough to apologize to Sandy for rushing off, and so he was gone and Jonathan was alone when Sandy touched Mr. Wellington.

He saw the concern in her eyes though she tried to hide it. "I'm going to just get him set up in his little environment," she said, as he hurried after her into her house. She told him to wait near the base of some stairs that she climbed hastily. Jonathan watched Sandy go, and when she was out of sight, he listened to her footsteps going up more stairs. He was standing near the dining room table where there were photographs in an open photo album of other animals that Sandy had helped. Some red squirrels, and other gray squirrels. Two possums.

It seemed a long time before she returned to tell him that Mr. Wellington's body temperature was far too low. She wanted to work with him right away. Try to get him settled; see if he'd eat some of the food she had. It was called rodent chow and was full of the nutrition he needed. His problem could be stress or he could be dehydrated or maybe he had a parasite. Hopefully he didn't have a serious problem.

Jonathan left. It was growing dark as he pedaled home, and along the way he stopped to put on his reflector vest and turn on the headlight on his bike. Most of the road was a two-lane through woods, winding and shadowed by the trees bunched along it. There wasn't a lot of traffic, but every now and then a car or truck came racing toward him with blinding lights, or rushed up behind him, and when they swept past, they seemed loud and big and he felt very small. He was worried that he'd kept the

squirrel too long. That he should have taken Mr. Wellington over to Sandy sooner. The instant she called. But he hadn't, and he knew it was because he had wanted to keep Mr. Wellington as a pet.

That night when his parents returned, he told them everything that had happened, and before going to bed, he e-mailed Sandy, thanking her for her help and asking her to please let him know how Mr. Wellington was doing. He tried to reach Vincent by instant message, wanting to make contact with someone who knew Mr. Wellington, but Vincent never answered, and Jonathan figured his brother was busy with that college paper he had to write. Jonathan had schoolwork, too, but he just couldn't concentrate.

In the morning an e-mail from Sandy waited:

The squirrel is mostly okay. But there is reason to worry. He has diarrhea, and that's not a good sign. I'm going to have the vet run a test in order to see if he has some kind of an infection or maybe parasites, or worms. He doesn't eat very much. Not as much as he should. There's a formula I could give him, which would supply nourishment, but I can't start him on this as long as he has diarrhea.

He wobbles, too, when he walks. His balance seems off, and at his age he should have more strength. It could be the dehydration.

CHAPTER THIRTEEN

 He awoke to new smells and a sense of danger. Though he could barely stand when he tried to move and explore, he kept trying. He had to try. Everything was different. He took a few steps, and then a few more. But suddenly his legs collapsed and he fell onto his belly. After some rest, he tried again and found there was a place to hide, a curving pile of wood that made a kind of cave. He could smell food and he was hungry, and then he saw the food. It was a short way ahead and he went to it. He nibbled and then chewed, but couldn't keep going without more sleep.

When he opened his eyes, he saw what looked like a

tree. He hadn't noticed it before, but as he woke this time, he sensed it, smelled it. He stirred and stood and saw it. When he got close, he found that it was small and didn't go anywhere, but it made him feel that his life might return to what it had been. At least it was possible. At least there was a tree. He slept and then woke to a wavering, shaking world and a blur of shapes flooding by and a strange, terrible smell, an overpowering smell, and forces that moved and lifted him and brought the smell closer and closer, trying to stick something into his mouth that he didn't want. He squealed and screamed

and tried to run, but his feet couldn't find the ground. And then he sailed down and away and was back in the world he'd just come to know with the tree and it was dark and he felt sad and scared. He hurried into the hiding place, and covered himself with his tail, hoping that the scary thing that had lifted him could no longer see him, would never find him again. He dozed for a while, but he was hungry again, so hungry he started walking almost without waking up back to the food he liked so much, where he crouched, eating and feeling hungry still, and eating more and more, feeling stronger, as he swallowed and nibbled and chewed, until he began to think that if the thing that had lifted him ever came again, he would be able to yell at it and tell it to get away from him and to stay away.

CHAPTER FOURTEEN

 The second e-mail from Sandy reported that Mr. Wellington didn't have worms. He didn't have parasites. But he was still weak. She remained worried.

A few days later she wrote again, describing how Mr. Wellington had refused to eat the formula she tried to give him by means of a feeding syringe. He had squealed and turned away and spit out the little she squirted into him. Jonathan could imagine Mr. Wellington not wanting the plastic dropper stuck into his mouth. But there was good news, too. It seemed that Mr. Wellington loved his rodent chow and ate it heartily.

A week or so later, on a Friday, Jonathan came home

from school late. He was tired and limping. His team had lost their hockey match, and he'd made a big mistake. He'd slipped and fallen and the boy he was guarding shot the winning goal. He'd been hit in the back of his leg by a stick, too, and that hurt, but the feeling of having failed his teammates was worse. The coach had told him not to worry. Many of his teammates had told him that he'd played a good game. But he felt bad. And the look in the eyes of a few of his teammates let him know that they felt, like he did, that he shouldn't have slipped and fallen.

He had a lot of homework but couldn't get started, turning on his computer and checking his e-mail instead, and seeing that there was one from Sandy. He opened it immediately and read:

Mr. Wellington continues to eat and he's starting to act like he knows he's the boss of his house! He scolds me and let's me know that he doesn't like me reaching into the cage, or even being too close. He really gives me a lecture about the fact that it's his territory. Which is all to the good. This is what we want from a healthy juvenile gray squirrel!

Also, I've learned that a friend of mine, who is a rehabber too and lives nearby, has a litter of grays that we think are close to Mr. Wellington's age. What we'd like to do is see if we can mix him into that litter, but we have to wait until he's a little stronger. It would be wonderful for him. He's very involved in grooming himself and he works hard to regularly clean his tail and his head. It's a skill he must have to stay healthy. Being with other grays his age would help him learn all the things he needs because of the way they learn from each other. He can pretty much handle breaking open acorns, which are softer than chestnuts, but he's still too young to break open a chestnut on his own, but when I give him one that's cracked a bit, he does the rest.

Jonathan hadn't realized how difficult it was to be a squirrel. He'd never thought for one second about all the skills a squirrel needed to have. And the fact that they had to learn these tasks amazed him. He'd always thought squirrels just knew the things they needed to know. But Mr. Wellington had to learn how to groom himself, and how to break open acorns and chestnuts. And his life depended on his learning these lessons.

Suddenly, hockey didn't seem so hard. Getting out his books and sitting down to his homework, he felt happy imagining the litter of other gray squirrels that Mr. Wellington would soon be moving in with.

But then on the very next day, Sandy wrote:

There may be trouble ahead, Jonathan. The idea of moving Mr. Wellington in with the other litter doesn't look so good. The time that has passed, which was necessary for him to get stronger, may have allowed them all to become too old. Mr. Wellington would be a complete stranger entering a litter that has been together from the beginning. He's territorial, and they will be too, and there can be real trouble sometimes. Not just arguing and scolding but actual violence.

As I wrote last time, Mr. Wellington is very possessive about his cage with me, and the other grays would be just as possessive about their house, maybe even more so. I fear we may just have to keep him alone. It's too bad, because he must be lonely.

CHAPTER FIFTEEN

It was a bright morning. He felt strong and bossy, climbing up on the little tree as far as he could go, which wasn't very far, but still it was a tree. Still, he was climbing. So he kept doing it. He went up and down and up and down and when he heard a noise, he scurried down to hide. Once things were quiet, he sneaked out for some food, which he carried back into his hiding place to nibble on. After a few seconds, he took what he hadn't eaten and hid it in a secret place where only he could find it. He felt smart and prepared in case he couldn't find food in the morning, and that made him blink almost contentedly as he went to sleep.

The next day was the same except for one thing. He felt stronger. And the next was the same as the one before except he felt stronger again, and then the next day he felt twice as strong. He hid away more food, and when the big shape came close to him, the other gigantic animal with the strange, unpleasant, dangerous smell, he yelled and screeched and said this little world he was in was his.

It belonged to him, and they, whoever they were, could have the world all around his little world but this was his, and he wanted that understood. He wanted to make that very clear, and he said it over and over in as sharp and strong a voice as he could find.

More days went by, more food, more growing strong and getting bigger, more jumping up on the little tree and hiding food away, more sleep and waking, more days and nights.

And then the world blurred, and he felt that he was floating, and though he scolded and argued, the big scary smell took him away, bouncing and bouncing, and when the hubbub finally stopped it had happened. The world had changed. There was no mistaking it. There were other squirrels. Three of them. And they looked at him. They waited and watched and seemed interested, and though he felt shy and though he felt fearful and though he felt angry that they might eat his secret food, still he was so excited he could barely breathe. Somehow his

cave had traveled with him to this new place, because he was inside it. He was crouched near his tree peering out of his doorway, and there they were. Three other squirrels. And he thought the right thing to do was just go about his business and not risk doing the wrong thing, and so he sank back inside his little cave and sat there wondering about his life, wondering about all that had happened, and as he was sitting and wondering, one of the other squirrels stuck his head in, and then this stranger walked in.

CHAPTER SIXTEEN

It was almost two months since they had taken Mr. Wellington to Sandy. It was late, and Jonathan was tired from hockey practice. They'd skated sprints and laps and more sprints and then practiced shooting and passing and done even more sprints. He'd come home with a lot of schoolwork, which had taken him hours to finish. He'd worked hard, taking breaks to listen to music and to instant message some friends. But all the while, he had been thinking about Mr. Wellington. It had been that way even at hockey practice. And when he climbed into bed, hoping to sleep, it was just the same. He had to wake up at seven in the morning in order to get to school

by eight, but he couldn't sleep. The big day was coming soon, the day when Mr. Wellington would go back out into the wild.

It was close to midnight when Jonathan returned once more to the e-mail he'd received from Sandy a week ago. The house was quiet. His dad and mom were both sleeping, as Jonathan read:

This morning I decided to give it a try. I took Mr. Wellington over to see if he could join the other litter. We put him into the cage with the three other gray squirrels and then we watched. Mr. Wellington had his own house, which I'd brought along and placed in the cage, and since everything else was new he stayed inside his house. He looked out once and then went back inside. He clearly wasn't sure what to do. One of the other squirrels saw him and just walked right into Mr. Wellington's house. We listened for sounds of a fight, but heard nothing; there wasn't even any chattering! They both stayed in there for a minute or two, and then Mr. Wellington walked out. I was pretty sure that the other gray was eating some of the snacks that Mr. Wellington had been putting away and storing up for his midnight snack attacks. Mr. Wellington strolled around the cage, looking things over, making a sort of thoughtful inspection, and then he went back into his house and he didn't seem troubled at all by the fact that the other gray was in there! When I peeked in they were curled up around each other so that it was hard to see whose tail was whose and they were sound asleep. So now he has brothers and sisters to play with, a family to help him learn all the things he needs to learn before they are all returned to the woods.

Maybe that was why he couldn't sleep, Jonathan thought, as he shut down his computer and made his way back to bed. Maybe it was because Mr. Wellington was going back into the wild. Or maybe he was out there right now and tonight was the night of the day he went. Or maybe it was the night before he would go. Whatever the case, Jonathan knew from Sandy how it would happen. How Mr. Wellington and the other squirrels would be put outside in a big pen with a locked gate. He and his

new littermates would be provided with food and water each day. They would have access to a tree trunk, or maybe a tree stump, and room to run and get used to the smells, the temperature, the wind. Once they were comfortable in this new place, the door would be opened. They could go if they wanted. They could go singly or together. The nearby tree line led into deep forest. They could stay in the woods or come back to the cage. The door would be left open and food would be provided.

For a while they would go and come back, go and come back, and then one day they would go but they would not come back.

Lying in his bed and sliding down from his day into sleep, Jonathan thought about Mr. Wellington off in the woods. And as he drifted off toward dreams, leaving behind his own running and playing and studying and "chattering" with friends, his own "grooming," he smiled, imagining Mr. Wellington now strong and full grown, with a big sweeping tail and big alert eyes, climbing a tree in the forest night. Clutching an acorn and climbing until he reached a limb, where he perched and cracked the acorn in his hands and ate the sweet meat he found inside. And with the moon shining in the star-filled sky behind him, and the breeze moving through his tail, and the acorn in his hands, Mr. Wellington was as contented and composed and serene and happy in the cold, wild dark of his high tree as Jonathan was, sinking into sleep in his bed.